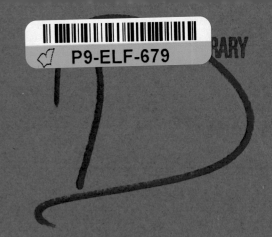

Three Perfect Peaches

A French Folktale retold by The Wild Washerwomen Storytellers,

Cynthia DeFelice & Mary DeMarsh

pictures by Irene Trivas

Orchard Books • New York

NOTE

As happens in the oral tradition of storytelling, tales change as they are passed from teller to listener and from generation to generation. We first heard this story from a friend and fellow storyteller, Cindy Peterson, and loved it. After searching for written sources of the tale, we finally discovered in *The Borzoi Book of French Folk Tales*, selected and edited by Paul Delarue (New York: Alfred A. Knopf, 1956), a story called "The Three May Peaches."

Mixing elements from that wonderfully earthy and humorous French tale with our memories of the story as we had heard it, we came up with the skeleton of the version you find here. Then the fun began! As we told and retold the story to people of all ages, it changed still more until we had made it our own. Now it's yours to tell and enjoy.

Text copyright © 1995 by Cynthia DeFelice and Mary DeMarsh

Illustrations copyright © 1995 by Irene Trivas

Orchard Books, 95 Madison Avenue, New York, NY 10016

Manufactured in the United States of America. Printed by Barton Press, Inc.
Bound by Horowitz/Rae. Book design by Mina Greenstein.
The text of this book is set in 14 point Granjon. The illustrations are watercolor reproduced in full color. 10 9 8 7 6 5 4 3 2 1

Library of Congress Cataloging-in-Publication Data
DeFelice, Cynthia C. Three perfect peaches : a French folktale / retold by the Wild Washerwomen
Storytellers, Cynthia DeFelice and Mary DeMarsh ; pictures by Irene Trivas.
p. cm. "A Richard Jackson book"—Half t.p.
Summary: The king offers his daughter's hand in marriage to the young man who can produce three perfect peaches.
ISBN 0-531-06872-2. ISBN 0-531-08722-0 (lib. bdg.)
[1. Fairy tales. 2. Folklore—France.] I. DeMarsh, Mary. II. Trivas, Irene, ill. III. Title.
PZ8.D35Th 1995 398.2'0944—dc20 [E] [20] 94-24872

For Stooby, the clever youngest brother

—C.D.

For
my mother, Lorraine
my children, Jenny and Tim
my family, Arnie, Mike, Molly, Martha—
and Dee!   —M.D.

For Mary and Ed Wendell —I.T.

*L*ong ago, in a faraway kingdom, there lived a red-haired princess who had a freckled face, a kind heart, and a clever mind. One evening when the princess went to bed, she was not feeling well, and in the morning she could not get out of bed. Her limbs were weak; her voice was faint; even her hair and her freckles were beginning to fade.

The king and queen called all the royal physicians to her bedside, but not one of them could figure out what ailed her. Her parents sat beside her, fearing the worst, when suddenly they heard her whisper, "If only I could have three perfect May peaches, I would be well again."

Word of the princess's desire was carried to the farthest corners of the kingdom, and many loyal subjects brought their finest peaches to the palace. But, alas, no peaches were quite perfect enough to cure the princess.

Finally, as his daughter drew close to death, the king grew desperate. He announced that he would give her hand in marriage to one who could find the peaches that would make her well. (In those days fathers, especially kings, could promise such things.)

A line formed outside the castle gate as all the young men in the kingdom appeared with their peaches, for all of them knew the princess, and all of them wanted to marry her.

Far out in the country there lived three brothers who had a peach tree growing by their door. When word of the king's announcement reached them, they, too, wished to try their luck at curing the princess. First the oldest brother went to the peach tree, picked three fine peaches, and set out for the royal palace. He hadn't gone very far when he met an old woman by the side of the road. He had never seen her before in his life, but she stopped him and said, "Tell me, grandson, what do you have in your basket?"

The oldest brother looked scornfully at the old woman and said rudely, "Why should I trouble myself to talk to you, you nosy old granny? But since you must know, there's nothing in my basket but rabbit droppings." "Very well," said the old woman. "Rabbit droppings it is, then."

The two of them went their separate ways. When the oldest brother arrived at the castle, he pushed his way to the front of the line and was taken to see the princess. He stepped up to her bedside and opened his basket to present his peaches. But, to his surprise, inside there were only rabbit droppings! The oldest brother was seized by the guards, thrashed soundly, and sent home in disgrace.

The next morning the middle brother went to the peach tree, picked three beautiful ripe peaches, and set out for the royal palace. He hadn't gone far when he, too, met the old woman by the side of the road and she said, "Tell me, grandson, what do you have in your basket?"

The middle brother sneered at the old woman and said, "Nosy, aren't you, granny? Well, if you must know, there's nothing in my basket but horse manure."

"Very well," said the old woman. "Horse manure it is, then."

The two of them went their separate ways. When the middle brother arrived at the palace, he pushed his way to the front of the line and was taken to see the princess. He stepped up to her bedside and opened his basket to present his peaches. But, to his amazement, inside there was nothing but horse manure! The middle brother was seized by the guards, thrashed soundly, and sent home in disgrace.

The youngest of the boys listened carefully to the tales told by his brothers. On the morning of the third day, he went to the peach tree and picked, not three, but four lovely peaches and set out for the palace. It was not long before he, too, met the old woman by the side of the road. She stopped him and said, "Tell me, grandson, will you, what do you have in your basket?"

The youngest brother tipped his hat politely and answered, "I have perfect May peaches, and I am going to marry the princess."

"Very well," said the old woman. "Perfect May peaches it is, then."

The youngest brother reached into his basket, took out a peach, and asked, "Would you like one?"

The old woman took the peach. "In return for your kindness," she said, "I'd like to give you this." She handed the youngest brother a silver whistle. "If ever you want anything, anything at all, just blow on the whistle and wish, and whatever you wish for will come to you all by itself. And if you should ever lose the whistle, simply clap your hands three times, and it will return to your pocket."

"Thank you," said the youngest brother, and the two of them went their separate ways. When the boy reached the castle, he took his place at the end of the line. At last he was taken to see the princess. He stepped up to her bedside and opened his basket.

When the princess saw his peaches, she sat up in bed. With the first bite of the first peach, the freckles returned to her cheeks. With the first bite of the second peach, her red hair began to sparkle with health. With the first bite of the third peach, she leaped out of bed and began to dance!

The king was indeed delighted at his daughter's recovery. But when he had finished rejoicing, he turned to look at the poor, shabby country boy who had cured her. He thought to himself, I must find a way to keep this marriage from taking place without appearing to break my promise.

To the youngest brother he said, "You've cured the princess and you shall have her hand in marriage. I *am* a man of my word. But first you must prove yourself worthy. I have a herd of one hundred rabbits. If you can tend them successfully, you may marry my daughter."

The youngest brother was sent out to a pasture with the rabbits.
He was told to keep watch over them all day long and, when evening came,
to herd them back to the palace. He was to do this, not one, but four days in
a row. If so much as one rabbit was found missing, he would fail in his task.

The youngest brother looked about him. There was no fence, no wall,
nothing to help him keep the rabbits together. One by one they hopped away,
leaving the youngest brother in despair.

But, late in the afternoon, he remembered the whistle. He blew on it and wished, and all one hundred of the royal rabbits came racing from the four corners of the kingdom! They formed a single-file line, snapped to attention, saluted smartly, and marched behind the youngest brother like soldiers following their general, all the way back to the castle door.

The king could not believe his eyes. He asked everyone who might have seen something, "*How* did he do it?"

A gardener who had been working in the pasture told the king about the silver whistle, and the king determined to obtain it for himself.

On the second day, without telling her why, the king sent his daughter out to the pasture with a sack of gold coins and instructions to beg, steal, or buy the whistle for her father. When the youngest brother saw the princess coming, he wondered what new obstacle the king was placing before him. For although he was poor and shabby, he understood many things, and he knew that the king wished him to fail.

When the princess offered to buy his whistle, he said, "Certainly, Your Highness. The price of my whistle is one hundred gold coins and one hundred kisses."

The princess handed over the one hundred gold coins without hesitation. But . . . she had never kissed a young man before. She looked into the youngest brother's eyes . . . and she liked what she saw. So she held up her face, puckered her lips, and the youngest brother kissed her one hundred times.

He handed her the whistle, she returned with it to the palace, and she gave it to her father.

Late that afternoon, when he was ready, the youngest brother clapped his hands three times and the whistle returned to his pocket. He blew on it and wished, and all one hundred of the royal rabbits came racing from the four corners of the kingdom! They formed a single-file line, snapped to attention, saluted smartly, and marched behind the youngest brother like soldiers following their general, all the way back to the castle door.

The king was *furious*! On the third day, he sent the queen out to the pasture with two sacks of gold and instructions to beg, buy, or steal the whistle for her husband. When the boy saw the queen coming, he said, "This is beginning to amuse me. . . ." And when the queen offered to buy the whistle, he said, "Certainly, Your Majesty, you may buy my whistle. The price today is two hundred gold coins and two hundred kisses."

The queen was a thrifty woman. Unhappily she handed over the two
hundred gold coins. But the queen was also a very lonely woman. The king was
so busy ruling the kingdom that he paid little attention to his wife . . . and so
she rather liked the idea of the two hundred kisses. She stepped up to the
youngest brother, wrapped her arms around him, and kissed him
two hundred times.

He handed her the whistle,
she returned with it to the palace,
and she gave it to the king.

But late that afternoon, when he was ready, the youngest brother clapped his hands three times and the whistle returned to his pocket. He blew on it and wished, and all one hundred of the royal rabbits came racing from the four corners of the kingdom! They formed a single-file line, snapped to attention, saluted smartly, and marched behind the youngest brother like soldiers following their general, all the way back to the castle door.

The king was nearly beside himself with rage. "I can see," he said, "that if I want this job done properly, I will have to do it *myself*!"

So on the morning of the fourth day, the king himself
rode out to the pasture on his horse, with a chest of gold
mounted atop the saddle. When the boy saw the king coming, he
smiled to himself. And when the king asked for the whistle, the boy
replied, "Certainly, Your Majesty, you may buy my whistle. The price
today is . . . let me see . . . three hundred gold coins . . . and . . . *YOU* . . .
WILL HAVE TO KISS YOUR HORSE'S BEHIND."

Furiously the king dismounted. He removed the chest of gold from the saddle and threw it at the boy's feet. Then he walked around to the other end of his horse. From his pocket he drew his handkerchief. He unfolded it carefully and held it up so that his royal handkerchief came in between his royal lips and his horse's royal behind. He puckered his lips and bent over, but . . .

"Ahem," said the youngest brother.

"Yes?" said the king scornfully.

"No," said the boy.

"No *what*?" asked the king.

"No handkerchief," said the boy.

"Really?" asked the king, his eyes wide with disbelief.

"Really," said the boy.

The king glared at the youngest brother and threw his handkerchief to the ground. Looking around to make sure that no one was watching, he kissed his horse's behind very quickly.

"*NOW GIVE ME THE WHISTLE,*" he demanded.

The boy handed it over, and the king returned to the palace. But late that afternoon, when he was ready, the youngest brother clapped his hands three times and the whistle returned to his pocket. He blew on it and wished, and all one hundred of the royal rabbits came racing from the four corners of the kingdom! They formed a single-file line, snapped to attention, saluted smartly, and marched behind the youngest brother like soldiers following their general, all the way back to the castle door.

The boy was greeted at the palace gate by the princess, the queen, the king, and the royal philosopher, who was the wisest man in the kingdom. The king said to the royal philosopher, "*You* tell him!"

The royal philosopher rubbed his hands together and said, "The king is a man of his word: you *shall* marry the princess. But first, there is one more task that you must perform to prove yourself worthy." He held up a crystal-clear glass bucket and said, "You must fill this bucket to overflowing with truth."

The youngest brother looked at the bucket and thought for a long moment. "All right," he said. "If it's truth you want, it's truth you shall have."

He stepped up to the princess, looked into her eyes, smiled, and said, "Is it true, princess, that I kissed you one hundred times?"

The princess smiled back at the boy and answered happily, "Yes, it's true."

"*WHAT?*" demanded the king.

"Is that enough truth for you?" asked the boy.

"Certainly not!" answered the king. "Look at the bucket. It's still quite empty."

"All right, then," said the boy, and he stepped up to the queen. "Is it true, Your Majesty, that *you* kissed *me* two hundred times?"

"Yes," whispered the queen, "it is true."

"WHAT?" cried the king.

"Is that enough truth for you?" asked the boy.

"Oh yes, I think that's quite enough truth for one day," said the queen anxiously.

"Not at all!" said the king. "Tell me more about the queen. I'm *fascinated*."

But instead the boy stepped up to the king. "Is it true, Your Majesty," he said, "that I, a poor, shabby country lad, made you, the king of all the realm, *kiss your horse's be—*"

"*IT'S A MIRACLE!*" shouted the king. "Everyone! Look at the bucket! The truth is overflowing and splashing onto the floor! *Say no more*, boy. *LET THE WEDDING BEGIN!!!*"

And so, the youngest brother and the princess
were married in May and they lived
happily ever after.